LICKETY-SPLIT

Robert Heidbreder

Dušan Petričić

Kids Can Press

To Sally, John, Wayne and Adam, too. Lovers of language, all — R.H.
For Irma, my newly arrived granddaughter — D.P.

Text © 2007 Robert Heidbreder
Illustrations © 2007 Dušan Petričić

Kids Can Press acknowledges the financial support of the Government of
Ontario, through the Ontario Media Development Corporation's Ontario Book
Initiative; the Ontario Arts Council; the Canada Council for the Arts; and the
Government of Canada, through the BPIDP, for our publishing activity.

Published in Canada by
Kids Can Press Ltd.
29 Birch Avenue
Toronto, ON M4V 1E2

Published in the U.S. by
Kids Can Press Ltd.
2250 Military Road
Tonawanda, NY 14150

www.kidscanpress.com

Acquired by Tara Walker and edited by Yvette Ghione
Designed by Dušan Petričić
Printed and bound in Singapore

This book is smyth sewn casebound.
CM 07 0 9 8 7 6 5 4 3 2 1

Library and Archives Canada Cataloguing in Publication

Heidbreder, Robert
    Lickety-split / written by Robert Heidbreder ; illustrated by Dušan Petričić.

ISBN 978-1-55337-710-8

1. Children's poetry, Canadian (English). I. Petričić, Dušan
II. Title.

PS8565.E42L52 2007   jC811'.54   C2006-906547-0

Kids Can Press is a *C*OrUS™ Entertainment company

LICKETY-SPLIT

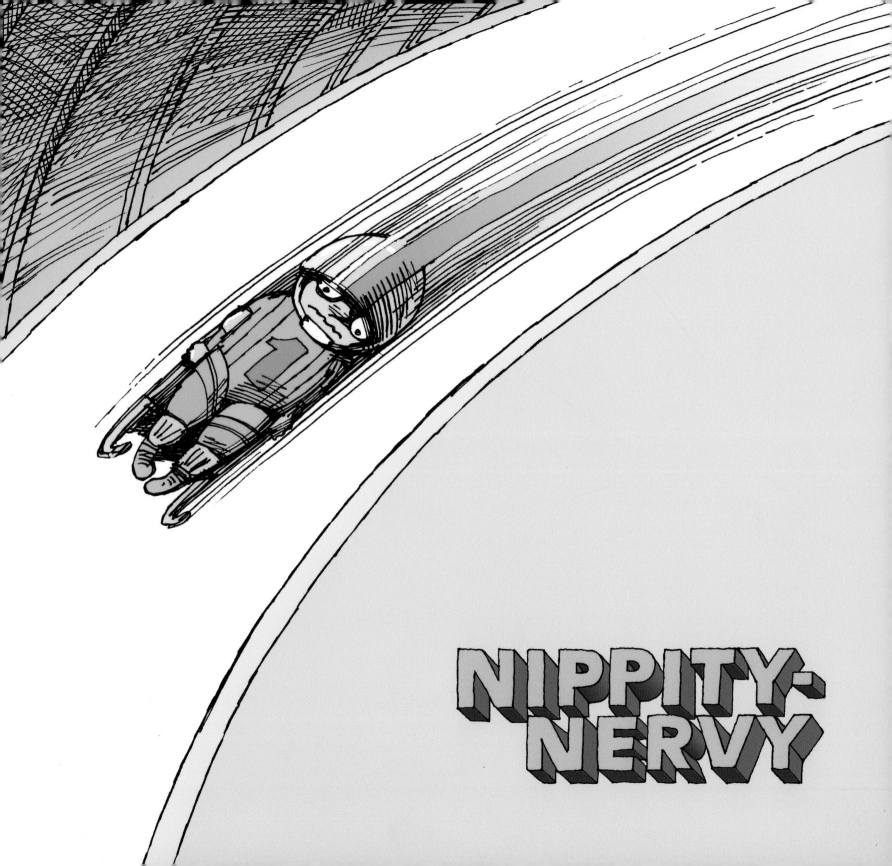

PLINKITY·
PLINKITY·
PLINKITY·
PLONK